This igloo book belongs to:

....

Published in 2013
by Igloo Books Ltd
Cottage Farm
Sywell
NN6 0BJ
www.igloobooks.com

Copyright © 2013 Igloo Books Ltd

All rights reserved. No part of this publication may be reproduced, stored in a retrieval system, or
transmitted in any way or by any means, electronic, mechanical, photocopying, recording or otherwise,
without the prior written permission of the publisher.

SHE001 0313
2 4 6 8 10 9 7 5 3 1
ISBN: 978-1-78197-007-2

Printed and manufactured in China

Animal Stories

igloobooks

Contents

Mousey Moves House

Mousey was moving out of the old barn. She wanted to live somewhere more exciting. Mousey hadn't gone far when she came across a big oak tree. "This would be a nice place to live," she thought, settling down for a rest in the shade.

6

Then, something landed on Mousey's head with a BUMP!
The naughty squirrels that lived in the tree were jumping from
branch to branch, dropping their acorns on Mousey's head.
"This isn't the right home for me," thought Mousey. "It's nuts!"

Mousey scurried into the grass nearby and came across a little burrow. "This looks cosy," she thought and ran down into the dark. Suddenly, she bumped straight into a big, brown rabbit. "This is MY burrow," said the rabbit. "Please leave!"

KEEP OUT!

Next, Mousey came to a little pond. Fish splashed in the rippling water and frogs hopped on their lily pads. "I'd love to live here," thought Mousey. She jumped onto the nearest lily pad, but she was much too heavy and slipped into the water with a SPLASH!

9

Sitting on the side of the pond, Mousey felt soggy and sad.
"None of these homes are right for me," she squeaked.
"Maybe you should try the field," croaked a little, green frog.
"I've heard there's a nice warm barn there."

"That's my old house," said Mousey to the frog. "I miss it very much."
So, she waved goodbye and set off towards the lovely, old barn in the field.
"There's nowhere else I'd rather be," said Mousey. "The barn is the perfect
home for a mouse like me!"

Brave Little Puppy

Dotty Puppy loved it when Mummy took her and her little brother, Patch, to the park. Dotty liked the slide and the swings but Patch thought they were frightening "What a scaredy-pup," said Dotty, teasing him. "Don't be mean to your brother," said Mummy.

Patch watched as Dotty whizzed down the big, red slide.
"Wheee!" she cried. "This is so much fun. You should have a go, Patch."
"No, thanks," said Patch, timidly. "I'll just stay down here."

13

Next, Dotty wanted to go on the yellow swings. "You can come too, Patch, if you're not too scared," she teased.

Patch watched his sister dash across the playground but he didn't follow her. The swings were where the older dogs played and he was too afraid to go there.

Suddenly, Patch heard Dotty yelp. He looked up and saw that she was stuck in the middle of the older dogs, who were running around and yapping loudly as they played. Dotty looked scared. Patch had to be a brave little puppy and rescue his sister.

Patch leapt up and raced towards his sister, with Mummy following close behind. "It's okay, Dotty, I'm here," he said. "We're sorry, we didn't mean to scare her," said the older dogs. "We were just playing."

"Don't worry," said Mummy, smiling. "Everyone feels scared sometimes, even the bravest little puppies."

Dotty was so proud of her little brother, she gave him a big hug. "You're my hero, Patch," she said, "and the best brother ever!"

17

Duck and Cluck

It was a hot, sunny day on the farm. "Let's go and cool off in the pond," said Duck to his best friend, Cluck. Duck waddled off and dived, SPLOSH, into the pond. "Come in, the water is lovely," he said, but Cluck just stood on the bank.

"I can't swim," said Cluck, looking sad. Some of the other ducks giggled behind their wings and Duck felt bad for his friend. Then, suddenly, he had a brilliant idea. "Wait right here," he said and waddled off towards the barn.

Inside the barn, there were lots of sawing and banging noises. The farm animals gathered around. They thought it was very strange and wondered what Duck could be doing. Then, the barn doors creaked open. "Surprise! I've made Cluck a boat!" cried Duck.

Duck and Cluck took the little boat down to the water.
"Jump in," said Duck. "We're going to have a great time together."
They rowed round and round the pond until they were dizzy.
Soon, the other animals wanted to join in, too.

Duck and Cluck held a diving competition and all the ducks dived off the side of the boat, one-by-one. Cluck waterskied behind the boat and Duck gave rides to the farm animals. "This is so much fun!" Cluck cried, happily.

Before long, everyone was having fun on the pond.

"Thanks for helping me, Duck. You've made my day," said Cluck.

"You're welcome," said Duck, smiling. "That's what friends are for. Now we can always have fun on the pond together."

The Best Bunny

Big Bunny always teased Little Bunny when they played in the garden. "I can jump higher than you," she boasted. "I bet you can't even jump over that yellow flower bush."

Little Bunny wanted to prove her wrong, so he had a go.

"Wheeeee!" cried Little Bunny as he flew upwards. "Aaaargh!"
he screamed, as he came back down and crashed into the bush.
Big Bunny laughed as she pulled him out. "If you can't jump
over the bush, you definitely won't be able to bounce over that
big puddle," she said.

With a single bound, Big Bunny soared across the water. "Your turn!" she said, turning around and grinning at him. Little Bunny took a hop, a skip and a jump and sprang forwards, but he landed halfway across the puddle with a loud, muddy, squelch!

"Now let's see who can hop the fastest," said Big Bunny. She raced to the end of the garden with Little Bunny scampering along behind her. He was trying so hard that he didn't see the stone in front of him. Little Bunny tripped and flew, straight through a hole in the vegetable patch fence.

Little Bunny felt sad, until he looked up and saw all the yummy vegetables around him. "Come in here, Big Bunny," he called. "There are lots of juicy carrots and plenty of lettuce to eat." "I can't!" cried Big Bunny. "I'm too big to fit through the fence."

"I can fit," said Little Bunny, smiling. He wiggled through the small hole easily, bringing a nice, big carrot for Big Bunny. "Thanks," she said, taking a bite. "Maybe being small isn't so bad after all!" After that day, she never made fun of his size again.

Farmyard Sports Day

It was a quiet day on the farm and the animals were bored. "If only there was something exciting to do," complained Cow.

Suddenly, Horse had an idea. "Let's have a sports day!" he said. The animals were very excited and couldn't wait to start.

First, was the egg and spoon race. The animals each lined up and Horse shouted, "Ready, steady, GO!" The eggs wibbled and wobbled and rolled away. Only Hen made it to the finishing line, flapping her wings and clucking away happily.

"Why don't we have a sack race next?" suggested Sheep.
He was great at sack races, but Cow got confused and put the
sack on her head. Goat started nibbling his and Pig fell into a
puddle. Poor Mouse was so small he got lost in his sack.

"Hurdles are much more fun," said Horse. He flicked his tail and flew over the fences at top speed. Pig decided that the hurdles were a bit too high and trotted around them instead. "I've got a great idea for the next event," he oinked.

Pig put the animals into two teams and gave them a long piece of rope to hold onto. "It's time for a tug of war!" he cried. The animals pulled and pulled as hard as they could, but neither team would budge. Then, Mouse gave an extra hard tug.

SNAP! The rope broke and the animals tumbled into a heap on the ground, laughing and giggling loudly. "I think that's a draw," clucked Hen, so Horse gave everyone a prize. "Our sports day has been so much fun," Hen said. "Let's do it all again next year!"

The Lost Nut

It was nearly dinnertime and Squirrel was feeling hungry, but she couldn't remember where she had hidden her nut. "It's not under the grey stone or in the strawberry patch," she said, searching her best hiding places.

Then, she saw something small and round hidden in the tree above. Thinking it was her nut, Squirrel scrambled up through the leaves and twigs. Suddenly, an angry mother bird swooped down, squawking, "Leave my egg alone!"

Squirrel ran away, but as she passed the pond she spotted her nut sitting on a lily pad. "I don't remember leaving it there," she thought, leaning over the water to grab it. SPLASH! The thing squirrel thought was her nut, hopped into the pond and swam away. It was actually a little, brown toad.

Squirrel was all wet and began to feel fed up. Her tummy was rumbling and she still couldn't remember where she had hidden her nut. Just then, a glimpse of something brown in the long grass caught her eye. "That must be my nut!" she cried.

Squirrel was so hungry, she bit straight into the nut with her sharp teeth. "OUCH!" cried a voice. It was Fox and his eyes were watering with pain. "That was my nose," he said.
"Sorry," squeaked Squirrel, and she scurried away quickly.

Squirrel ran home as fast as her little paws would go.
"I'll be safe here," she thought as she dived into bed.
Then, she felt something small and round under her pillow.
"It's my lost nut!" cried Squirrel. "This is where I left you."
At last, Squirrel could enjoy eating her nut.

41

The Music Contest

In the Cherry Blossom tree, the birds were busy practising for the big music contest. They whistled and warbled, tweeted and trilled, but one bird was not singing. Baby Bird perched on the end of a branch and sighed.

"I wish I could sing like the other birds," he said, sadly, but every time Baby Bird opened his beak, a little squawk came out. "Don't worry," cooed Dove. "All birds can sing. Just open your beak nice and wide like me and you'll sound wonderful, I'm sure."

43

So, Baby Bird opened his beak as wide as he could and started to sing, but out came a terrible screech! Dove covered her ears in fright. "Maybe you should practise singing somewhere else," she twittered and the other birds agreed.

Baby Bird flapped sadly to a nearby tree where Spider was spinning a web. "Oh, Spider," he said. "I'm such a bad singer, I'll never be able to join in the music contest with the other birds." "You don't have to sing to make music," said Spider, kindly. "Come on, I'll show you."

Spider asked Baby Bird to collect some nutshells and twigs and got to work spinning several long strings. Before long, she had made Baby Bird a cool guitar. When Baby Bird plucked the strings they made a lovely noise. "Wow, thanks Spider," he said.

On the day of the big music contest, Baby Bird felt nervous as he waited to go on stage. All the other birds took turns to tweet and chirp their sweet songs. When it was Baby Bird's turn to perform, he burst onto the stage and played his special guitar.

The birds were amazed. They had never heard anything like Baby Bird's marvellous music. They danced along as he played and cheered loudly when Owl awarded him the winner's trophy.

Baby Bird was so glad he had taken part even though he was different to the other birds. It was the best day ever.